This book belongs to

_____

_____

For
Wilbur
Jones

First published 2020 by Macmillan Children's Books
This edition published 2021 by Macmillan Children's Books
an imprint of Pan Macmillan
The Smithson, 6 Briset Street, London EC1M 5NR
EU representative: Macmillan Publishers Ireland Ltd, 1st Floor,
The Liffey Trust Centre, 117–126 Sheriff Street Upper,
Dublin 1, D01 YC43
Associated companies throughout the world.
www.panmacmillan.com

ISBN: 978-1-5290-2138-7

3 5 7 9 8 6 4 2

A CIP catalogue record is available for this book from the British Library.

Printed in Poland

Just One of
Those Days

Jill Murphy

MACMILLAN CHILDREN'S BOOKS

It had been a long night . . .

. . . so Mr and Mrs Bear woke up late.

They left Baby Bear dreaming
of dinosaurs while they got ready
for work.

Then they woke Baby Bear and
got him ready for Nursery, which
took even longer than usual.

Outside, it was raining. Mr Bear got
the bus and Mrs Bear took Baby Bear
to Nursery on her way to work.

Nursery had already started by the time
they got there.

In the cloakroom, Baby Bear wouldn't
take his coat off.

"I want to go home," he said, in a very
small voice.

Mrs Bear took Baby Bear to join the class.

His teacher was reading them a story.

"*There* you are!" she said. "In you come."

After the story, Baby Bear saw that
Someone Else was playing with his
best dinosaur.

"MINE!" he yelled.

"No, no," said his teacher. "Come and play
with Diplodocus instead. He's just as nice."
Baby Bear tried hard to like Diplodocus,
but his mouth didn't open and he didn't
have purple blotches – so it was difficult.

At work, Mrs Bear sat on her glasses and Mr Bear spilt coffee all over an important pile of papers.

At Nursery, when it was lunchtime, Someone Else got the red cup. The water didn't taste as nice in the green one.

At work, Mr Bear didn't have time for lunch. He was too busy reprinting the messed-up papers – and Mrs Bear fell asleep half-way through her blueberry muffin.

At Nursery, after lunch they did painting, which was nice, but Someone Else had used all the purple paint.

Then they did cooking, which got a bit messy.

Then they did dancing, which got a bit tricky.
"I want you all to dance like trees in the wind," said their teacher.

By the end of the day, Baby Bear could
hardly keep his eyes open. He was so
glad to see his Mum waiting for him.
It was still raining as they trudged
home together.
"Daddy's bringing in a pizza," said Mrs Bear,
"so we don't have to cook."
When they got home, Mrs Bear and
Baby Bear got into their comfy pyjamas.

"Daddy's home!" yelled Baby Bear.

Mr Bear came in, with a big pizza box
and a carrier bag.

"Look in the bag," he said. "It's something
for you."

Baby Bear dived into the bag and brought out
– T. Rex!

"He's exactly the same as the one you always
play with at Nursery," said Mr Bear proudly.
"I saw him in a shop window and thought you
might like to have one of your very own."

Baby Bear tested the jaw to make sure
it moved. Then he hugged Mr Bear
very tightly.
Then he took off the labels.

Then he and T. Rex roared, and chased
Mum and Dad into the kitchen.
"Better get this pizza on to plates,"
said Mrs Bear, "before *someone* goes
into orbit!"

"How was work?" asked Mr Bear, as they made their way to the sofa with their pizza. "Not brilliant," said Mrs Bear. "How about you?"

"Not brilliant," said Mr Bear. "I think it was just one of those days."

"Never mind," said Mrs Bear. "We can have a better one tomorrow – why don't we all go to bed early?"

"Good idea," said Mr Bear. "I'll do the bedtime story . . ."

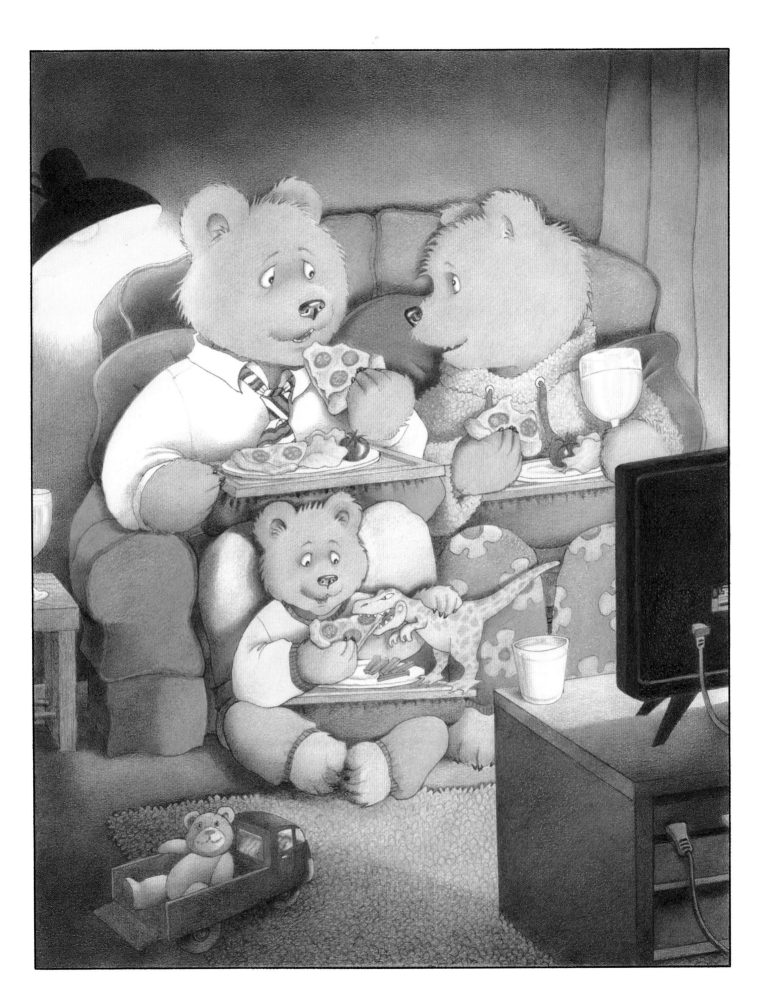

. . . and he did.

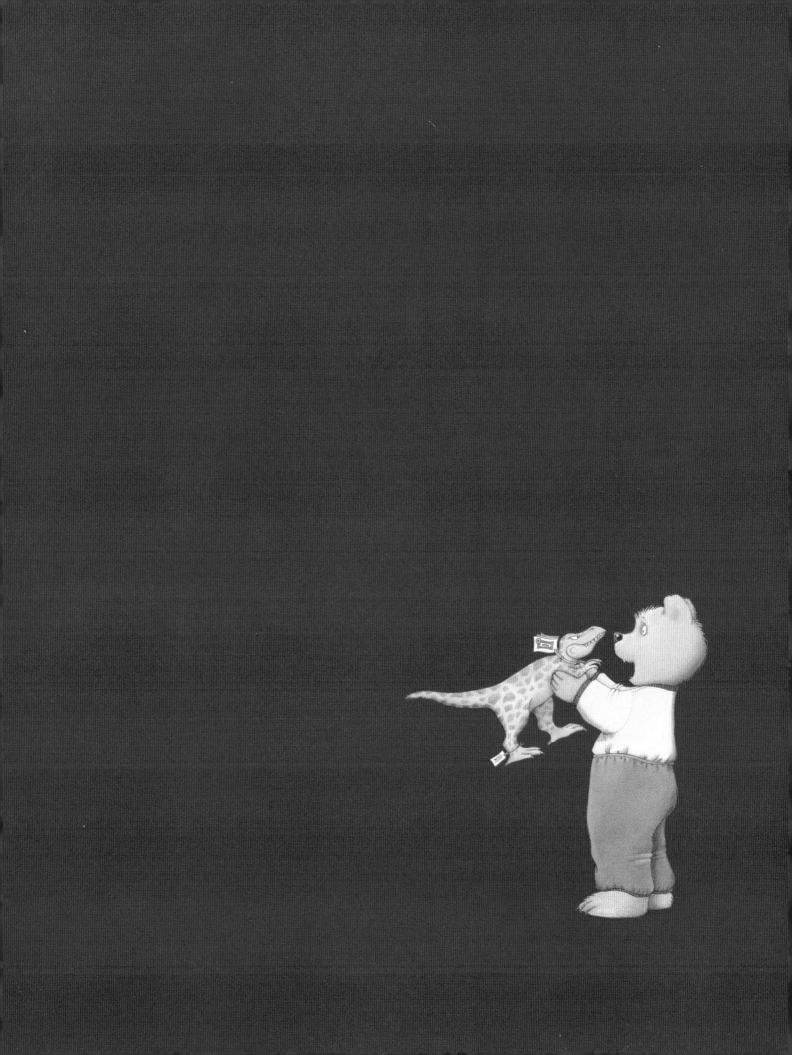